This book belongs to…

_____

_____

Pronunciation Guide

Adha: Aa-dhaa

Chand: Chaand

Eid: Eed

Eidi: Ee-dee

Farnaz: Fur-naaz

Fitra: Feet-raa

Iftar: If-taar

Jama Masjid: Juh-maa Mus-jeed

Khala Eidet: Khaa-laa Ee-date

Khurma: Khoor-maa

Milan: Mee-lun

Mubarak: Moo-baa-ruk

Ramadan: Ruh-maa-daan

Salaam: Suh-laam

Suhoor: Su-hoor

Tumbilotohe: Toom-bee-lo
-toe-hay

Zakir: Zaa-keer

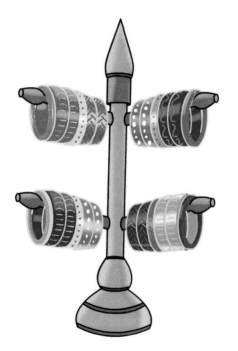

Note for parents: Our books provide a glimpse into the beautiful cultural diversity of India, including occasional mythology references. Ramadan and Eid are celebrated in many different ways across India and the world. In this book, we showcase elements of Ramadan and Eid that are best suited for young readers to follow.

Maya & Neel's India Adventure Series, Book 4

Let's Celebrate Ramadan & Eid!

Muslim Festival of Fasting & Sweets

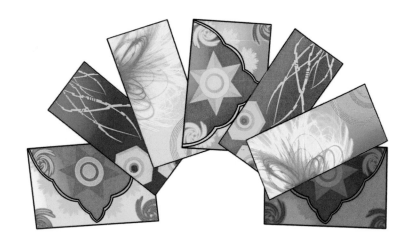

Published by: Bollywood Groove
www.BollyGroove.com/books

Written by:
Ajanta & Vivek

Edited by:
Janelle Diller

Special Thanks:
Asma Afridi, Michelle Yousuf,
Sakina Fakhruddin, Sheila Gilani

This is a map of India. India is a big country. It has many states, languages, festivals, and dances.

Do you see the red spot on the map? That's New Delhi.

Many Muslims live in India including in New Delhi.

Muslims celebrate Ramadan and Eid festivals all over India and the world.

Maya & Neel arrive in India and meet their friends Farnaz and her older brother, Zakir. They also meet Khan Uncle & Aunty, Farnaz and Zakir's Mom and Dad.

"Salaam Maya & Neel. Hello. Great to see you!" Farnaz says.

"Salaam. Thank you for inviting us to celebrate Ramadan and Eid with you. We are so excited!" Maya & Neel reply.

"So what exactly are Ramadan and Eid?" Maya asks. "Let me tell you," Khan Aunty says.

What are Ramadan & Eid?

Ramadan is a special month in the Muslim calendar. During Ramadan, we fast for thirty days.

Fasting means not eating or drinking. So, do we stay hungry all day?

No. We eat before sunrise...

...but don't eat or drink all day...

...and then we eat again after sunset.

Why do we fast? Many poor people around us do not have enough to eat. Ramadan makes us think about those poor people and feel thankful for all we have.

Even if you are too young to fast, you can still celebrate Ramadan by giving up something you love, such as candy or a favorite toy.

Eid is the day after Ramadan ends. We celebrate with prayers, yummy food and other fun stuff. Muslims actually celebrate two big Eids.

This one is called Eid-Al-Fitr and also known as Sweet Eid. Can you guess from the picture why? The other Eid is called Eid-Al-Adha.

Rrrrriiinnng the alarm clock sounds next morning. Maya's & Neel's eyes pop open. But it's still dark outside.

Zakir calls out "Time to wake up". "Nooooo!" Farnaz says. "I want to sleep more." "It's time for our *Suhoor* meal!" Zakir reminds her.

"What's *Suhoor*?" Neel asks. "It's the meal before sunrise. For those who fast, this is the only time they will eat before sunset".

"Oh, right" Farnaz jumps out of bed. "I don't want to miss all the yummy food".

Zakir munches on dates. He declares "I want to fast this year". "Yes, you are now old enough to do that" Khan Aunty agrees.

"And how about me?" Farnaz asks. "Not yet, but you can give up something you like a lot," Khan Uncle replies.

"I won't eat any candy or play with my favorite teddy bear for the next thirty days" Farnaz says.

Farnaz looks very serious.

"I am so proud of you, Farnaz, and you too, Zakir" Khan Uncle says.

"We would love to do the same" Maya & Neel add. "To celebrate Ramadan, we won't eat any candy for the next thirty days."

"And no peanut for me" Chintu chirps.

As the day goes by, Zakir gets hungry. But he holds strong. The rest of the kids have a quiet and quick lunch.

"Zakir, how are you able to not eat or drink all day?" the kids ask.

"It's not so hard when I think of all the children around the world who don't have enough to eat.

That's the whole idea behind Ramadan." Zakir replies with a smile.

The day ends and the sun sets. The family once again gets together.

Khan Aunty calls out, "Zakir, time for *Iftar*, or breaking your fast".

Mom, Dad and Zakir have dates and water to break their fast.

Then they all have a tasty dinner.

A few days later, Khan Uncle and Aunty ask everyone to join them on a drive to a local shelter.

It's a large building where a lot of poor people live who don't have much money.

The kids walk into a giant dining hall where people are lined up to get food.

"A big part of Ramadan is helping those who need it the most." Khan Uncle explains.

"Kids, you get to help serve food while we work in the kitchen". The children all quickly stand behind food tables and start serving food.

People give the kids lots of thanks and wish them well. The children and even Chintu feel very happy.

The last night of Ramadan finally arrives. Khan aunty tells them, "Tonight is called *Chand Raat* or the night of the moon. Ramadan ends tonight. Lets head to the market and buy new clothes."

The kids are excited. They head over to a colorful market.

Farnaz says, "Maya, try on some of those bangles."

"Sure!" Maya says.

"And what are you putting on your hand?".

"It's a paste called *Henna*. You can draw pretty patterns with it on your hand," Farnaz says. The boys pick up some cool new clothes for themselves.

The next morning everyone wears white or light colored clothes.

Khan Aunty tells them, "Today is Eid. We will start the day by going to a famous mosque called Jama Masjid and do a special prayer for Eid."

"What is a mosque?" Maya asks.

"A mosque is where Muslim people pray. Jama Masjid is one of the most famous mosques in the world!" Khan Aunty says.

Maya & Neel ask, "Should we wear our new clothes now?"

"No, we wear plain and light colored clothes now. We'll dress up only after Eid prayer is done.

This is so that everyone feels equal in the mosque—no matter how rich or poor they are."

After praying at the Jama Masjid, they meet outside and hug each other. "Eid *Mubarak!* Happy Eid."

Farnaz and Zakir are very excited. "Now it's time for Eid feast! Let's have lunch!" they exclaim.

They come home and change into their Eid clothes. They all sit down at a table full of tasty food.

"Yum! This smells delicious," Neel says. They pass chicken rice and kababs to each other.

"This looks like spaghetti in milk," Maya giggles and points to a bowl.

Neel puts a little on her plate.

"This is called *Sheer Khurma*. It is the special food for Eid. It's made out of *Seviyan*, or thin pasta and lots of milk," Zakir says.

The kids finish every last bit of the yummy food!

"Time for your *Eidi*," Khan Uncle says. He gives them each a special envelope, which all kids get on the day of Eid. Chintu gets a box of nuts.

Maya and Neel eagerly open their envelopes. "Oh wow! There's money inside! What should we do with it?

Zakir says, "How about we pool it together? We use half of the money to buy something we can all use. And we give the rest to someone who is poor?" "Great idea!" everyone says.

Khan Aunty takes more envelopes in a bag. "Kids, let's head out for Eid *Milan* and meet family and friends. We'll wish them Eid *Mubarak*. Let's not forget to take some sweets with us!"

They arrive at Zakir and Farnaz's uncle's house.

They eat more food and *Sheer Khurma*. Uncle hands them more *Eidi*. "Our money pool is getting bigger!" the kids exclaim.

Uncle introduces them to other guests who are from all around the world — Saudi Arabia, Somalia, Indonesia and Afghanistan.

"Will you please tell us how Eid is celebrated in your country?" Maya asks the guests.

Eid around the world

In Saudi Arabia, people leave bags of rice outside the house of those who don't have much money.

In Somalia, some people celebrate Eid by doing a traditional dance.

In Indonesia, people light traditional torches to welcome Eid. This ceremony is called *Tumbilotohe*.

In Afghanistan, kids go from house to house saying, "*Khala Eidet Mubarak.*" They receive cookies called *Pala*.

"That was so much fun! Ramadan and Eid are such beautiful festivals!"
Neel says.

"I agree. I also loved the idea of helping poor people during
Ramadan." Maya adds.

"We cannot wait for our next adventure. We wonder where that will
be. We hope you can join us then," Maya, Neel and Chintu say.

"Until then, *Salaam!*"

Let's look back on our wonderful Ramadan & Eid Celebrations...

What do people not do
during Ramadan?
*Don't eat or drink from
sunrise to sunset*

How long is Ramadan?
Thirty days

What is *Suhoor*?
*Meal before
sunrise*

What is *Iftar*?
Meal after sunset

What is something we
do during Ramadan?
Help poor people

What is the last night of
Ramadan called?
Chaand Raat

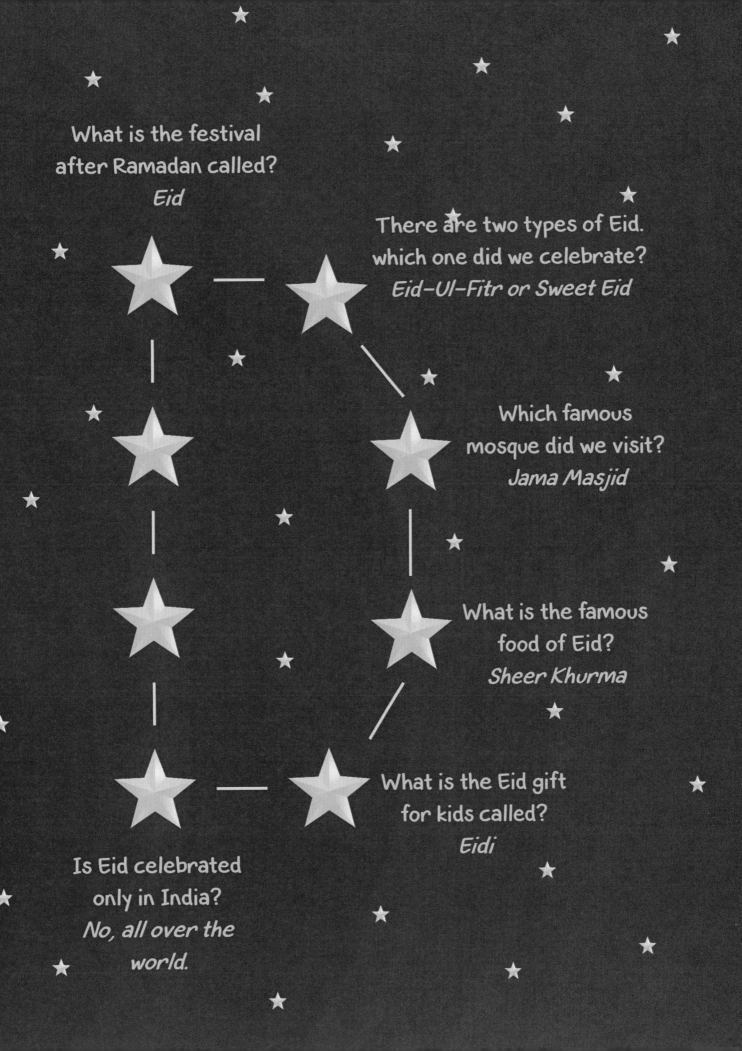

About the Authors:

Ajanta Chakraborty was born in Bhopal, India, and moved to North America in 2001. She earned an MS in Computer Science from the University of British Columbia and a Senior Diploma in Bharatanatyam, a classical Indian dance, to feed her spirit.

Ajanta quit her corporate consulting job in 2011 and took the plunge to run Bollywood Groove full-time. The best part of her work day includes grooving with classes of children as they leap and swing and twirl to a Bollywood beat.

Vivek Kumar was born in Mumbai, India, and moved to the US in 1998. Vivek has an MS in Electrical Engineering from The University of Texas, Austin, and an MBA from the Kellogg School of Management, Northwestern Univ.

Vivek has a very serious day job in management consulting. But he'd love to spend his days leaping and swinging, too.

Our Story:
We are co-founders of **Bollywood Groove™ (bG),** a Bollywood dance and fitness company for kids and adults. We started bG in 2008 in the Bay Area, California and then re-started it in 2011 after we moved to Chicago.

We barely knew a soul in Chicago but were overwhelmed by the warmth and support of our loving Chicago community who showed a very strong interest to learn about and experience Indian culture. We slowly built bG from 1 to 30+ classes per week.

When we started our **bG Kids! Program (ages 2-15)** in 2011, we wanted our classes to be more than just dancing to popular Bollywood songs. We aspired to make our classes educational and to introduce our students to the rich and diverse culture of India in addition to learning a dance choreography.

To this effect, we introduced **CultureZOOM**, an immersion into Indian culture, that is taught in each class via fun activities — storytelling, games, craft projects and mini-plays. CultureZOOM has been very well received! Kids (and even parents) are excited to learn more about India and its rich cultural heritage. Over the years we have refined our approach and continue to test the content in our classes.

This book series is a way to share this content with a broader audience and we hope young readers will enjoy a glimpse into the beautiful cultural diversity that makes up India.

In our spare time — who are we kidding? We have a two-year-old toddler. Dancing, running Bollywood Groove, writing books, and chasing our very rambunctious child is all that we can fit in a day!

Our Titles: 3,000+ SOLD! (avail. on Amazon worldwide)

Check out our website for more kids books
www.BollyGroove.com/books

Made in the USA
Lexington, KY
21 May 2018